VAMPIRE OF THE SUN

S.T. CARTLEDGE

ERASERHEAD PRESS
PORTLAND, OREGON

ERASERHEAD PRESS
833 SE Main St. #342
Portland, OR 97214

www.eraserheadpress.com

ISBN: 978-1-62105-327-9
Copyright © 2023 by S.T. Cartledge
Cover art copyright © 2023 conejo_rosa
Cover design copyright © 2023 by Rose O'Keefe

Printed in the USA.

VAMPIRE OF THE SUN

For Kim, who has taken up this adventure into parenthood by my side.

For Lily, I wrote this while you were sleeping in my arms.

PART ONE:
FIRST DAYS

I

The sun was a dragon spitting fire out into space, and from its burning maw there escaped a tiny fleck of burning gas containing the very essence of life. It came hurtling towards earth, which was not a dragon, but a very strange rock filled with very strange life forms.

II

Chloe cried the whole night the first night she was in hospital alone. She imagined crying herself to sleep, but the sleep never came. The midwives promised that they would come and visit her throughout the night but they never did. The baby cried so much she thought her ears would burst. She thought her heart would burst from the guilt of having this precious creature that she wanted so badly but now she felt hopeless and lost.

Why did no-one tell her it would feel like this? Why did no-one take her under their wing and tell her that it would feel like shit for now but that it would be okay?

Give it some time and you will be okay. Squeeze my hand, I'm right here and I love you. The voice of her husband, Malcolm, echoed in her head and felt like the only thing keeping her sane.

She watched the wall clock tick over the minutes, waiting for the morning visiting hours to come so she could hear his voice again for real, so he could hold Sabrina close to his heart and soothe her.

Chloe tried to sleep in the hospital during the day, but suddenly the midwives were in and out every other minute, talking her through shit she barely paid attention to, going over some things she'd heard a thousand times, ran her through all the worst-case scenarios for her little baby girl and how to prevent this or that fatal occurrence, but they only managed to burrow her insecurities and fears deeper into her mother-brain, such that she felt like she would never recover.

The second night alone was worse than the first. The lack of sleep was driving her crazy, but every time there was a moment's peace and she was at the point of falling asleep, now was the time the goddamn midwives came to check on her and set the baby off in a screaming frenzy.

The next morning she checked out against the doctor's recommendation, and with a prescription to manage the pain from her cesarean, she felt some glimmer of hope that home would offer her some semblance of comfort and peace.

After a slow and careful drive home (Malcolm clutched the steering wheel so tight) Chloe practically passed out on the couch while Malcolm rocked Sabrina gently to sleep.

Neither mother nor child woke to the sound and the shudder of the small projectile of burning star colliding with the earth in their back yard. Malcolm placed the sleeping babe down in her bassinet and went outside to investigate.

III

Malcolm turned the garden hose on full blast and reeled it out from the wall, aiming it at the smouldering crater in the yard. The grass singed an amber glow against the charred black earth and as Malcolm approached the hole, he saw the burning projectile within, a bright white lump which steamed and sizzled as the water hit its skin.

The water spat and the steam rose in thick clouds and as the water pooled in the hole, the water boiled, crackling loud and bubbling and as the water level rose, the lump floated, spinning and spitting and glowing in the hole.

Malcolm noticed a high pitch squeal coming from the thing, which persisted as the water cooled and the steaming and spitting died down. At first it sounded like a kettle at boiling pressure, a whistling spout, but as it continued Malcolm realised that it wasn't the steam making the noise, but the thing itself. It reminded him of something else deeply nestled in his mind.

"Sabrina" he whispered, noticing the cry like that of his newborn child. "Sabrina" he said, louder this time, dropping the hose and letting it whip violently back into its reel. He stumbled to the hole's edge and dipped his hands into the water. It was warm, but not scalding. He submerged them to his forearms, scooping up the little ball in his large arms and the high pitch squeal became an unrelenting scream.

IV

It wasn't Sabrina, of course. Malcolm knew that, but he also felt a part of his paternal brain willing to play tricks on him. This crater baby sounded like his daughter. It looked kind of like his daughter, but with white skin instead of a mocha brown. He gently rolled it over in his arms and noticed two things. First, that it was a boy. Second, that it had two little horn-like bone growths on its skull, not to mention the super small, super fine razor sharp teeth already occupying its mouth.

Malcolm made a mental note not to put his finger anywhere near its mouth, and definitely not let it near a mother's lactating bosom. The baby screamed and squirmed so violently Malcolm felt hopeless to comfort it.

The back door slid open and Chloe stood there in a sleepy daze and muttered, "bring her to me, she's hungry." She noticed not the baby's skin or its horns and teeth, its exposed willy. Only the scream which filled the neighbourhood and proceeded to bleed out into the sky.

Malcolm handed the baby over to Chloe and said "I found this in the crater."

"What," she muttered, still stirring from her fatigue. She unclipped her nursing bra to feed the crying babe.

"It came from the crater, babe," he replied. "That's not Sabrina, that baby's got teeth."

"Does she seem hot to you? I think she's got a fever," she said.

"Babe," he touched her arm, curling his fingers around her and holding her from feeding this unnatural beast baby. "Stop, babe. Stop."

She stepped back and stared at him in somewhat of a daze.

He stared right back and said, "This. Is. Not. Our. Child."

Now seeming more alert, Chloe looked down at the crying baby and startled herself at the sight of him. He had felt so soft and natural in her arms, he certainly felt like her child. Even Malcolm noticed she looked more comfortable holding him than she did her own offspring, and the baby itself cried less than it did with Malcolm.

"Whose baby is it then? How come you had it?" she said, coming around to the illogical truth of it all.

"No idea," he replied. "Like I said, I found it in the crater."

Chloe noticed the crater full of water for the first time, its steam was still rising and the burnt black earth had a glossy sheen to it now.

From inside the house Sabrina's cries rang out and Malcolm went in to fetch her. Chloe stood in the back yard with this new baby, gently rocking side to side, gazing into its bright golden eyes and taking note of all the ways it looked like her daughter and all the ways it looked different. Where she should have felt fear or confusion, she only felt love. This little ball of warmth pulsed gently in her arms and fell into a deep slumber.

She thought he was perfect in every single way.

V

Malcolm had Sabrina sleeping in his arms as he sat in the lounge room, Chloe had the other baby sleeping on her in the rocking chair.

"What do you think of the name Icarus?" she said in a projected whisper across the room.

"To be honest, it makes me nervous," Malcolm said. "This thing in your arms, we can't name it. We've got no idea what it is or where it came from."

"Yes, my love, but this poor helpless creature came to us. He needs us," she said. The little comet-baby lay peacefully on her chest, oblivious to the debate unfolding in the room around him.

"He needs professional medical help, is what he

needs, Chloe," Malcolm snapped. "We can only barely manage things with one child, we've got no chance with two. We have to put this baby in a home that can afford to support it. That's the best thing for it and the best thing for us."

"I can't," she said. "I can't give him up. He's just so sweet and perfect. I love him."

Malcolm let out an exhausted and frustrated sigh. "I'm just trying to think of our future," he said.

"And I'm not?" Chloe snapped.

"I didn't mean..." he replied.

It was Chloe's turn to sigh. She held a hand over the baby's ears so her talking wouldn't wake him. He squirmed a little, but remained asleep. "It's just, holding him for the first time felt like family. I felt that connection. I saw that future and it filled me with hope, with joy."

Malcolm patted Sabrina gently and listened.

"When I hold Sabrina I just feel so un-motherly. Like, all she does is cry and scream and I try anything, I try everything to comfort her, and nothing works and..." tears began to well in her eyes, "and I was thinking is this how it's meant to be? Is it supposed to feel like this? Or am I just a bad mother?"

"You're not a bad mother, babe, you've just been put through the wringer these past few days. Give it time and you'll get there. We'll get there... As a family."

"But how can I go from Sabrina to this little baby and it's the complete opposite? How is this a thing?"

The baby made a murmur in her arms and squirmed some more. They were talking too loud.

"I don't know, I mean, he came from a crater in the ground. He's not a natural born child, Chloe." Malcolm dropped his voice back down, patting and rocking Sabrina while she fought in his arms to wake up. "Let's just give it a bit of time before we decide what to do, hey." Malcolm shot Chloe a supportive smile. "And I like the sound of Icarus. Why wasn't it on our list of baby names?"

Chloe wiped her tears on her sleeve and held the warm little Icarus to her chest and for the moment she felt like she would be ok.

VI

That night it felt like the world was ending. From the moment the sun went down Icarus started to cry again. With breastfeeding out of the question for him, Chloe and Malcolm tried to give him formula, but he wouldn't take it.

His body temperature plunged rapidly and he broke out into a cold sweat. His flesh was clammy to the touch, and no matter how much they rugged him up, no matter how many layers of clothes and how many blankets they wrapped him in, his forehead still felt cold as ice and his cries were relentless.

Of course, this set Sabrina off in a panic too, but there were brief moments of relief for one parent when

Sabrina settled a little when they kept the babies on opposite ends of the house.

They met momentarily to swap between Sabrina and Icarus, with Malcolm passing Sabrina to Chloe to feed, and her passing Sabrina back to sleep, and there was the rare moment when Malcolm put Sabrina down to sleep, that he and Chloe could continue to try to comfort Icarus together.

Those moments didn't last long.

It was in the early hours of the morning when time was really exercising its elasticity, stretching and blurring in ways that Malcolm and Chloe had no idea what the actual time was, at the point right before they would be overcome by complete overwhelming hopelessness, when silence fell upon the household.

Chloe had just been trying to feed Sabrina for what felt like the fifth time in about an hour and a half, and the poor child was so exhausted from crying and feeding and crying and feeding, that she had fallen asleep on Chloe's boob.

Chloe had expected to hear Icarus' screams echoing throughout the halls, but she heard only silence, the ringing in her ears was just a lingering projection of the past few hours, the past few days.

Chloe started crying, although she couldn't tell whether it was from relief or exhaustion or what. She wandered the house until she found Malcolm in the bathroom, holding Icarus with his arms outstretched, the baby stripped of his blankets and clothes, of all but his nappy, and glowing beneath the full power of the heat lamps.

Malcolm had been thinking for hours about questioning Chloe's will to keep this child, performing the mental gymnastics around finding the balance between a cruel and heartless 'I told you so' and a rational list of why this child needs to be left in a basket outside the hospital in the morning. Then he felt it too, the love and longing to raise this child as his own. That peace bringing about such an intense connection, that there could be no other parents for this child. And Malcolm had completely forgotten all the conversations in his head about giving him up.

Yes, it would be harder than anything they'd ever had to do in their lives a million times over, but he wouldn't have it any other way. Chloe came up to him and wrapped her arms around his waist. He was overheating under the heat lamps and sweat beaded on his bald black scalp, trickling down his face. His eyelids were so heavy they were begging for sleep, but the relief of silence and the overwhelming emotion of love he felt for Icarus, for his whole family, caught him off guard and he too began to cry.

VII

Chloe sat in the rocking chair after giving Sabrina her feed, and patted the baby's back to help her burp. Sabrina let out a long, loud burp, along with a chunk of regurgitated milk into the burp cloth in Chloe's hand.

"Malcolm, babe, can you get in here?" Chloe called out.

He sensed the panic in her voice, and rushed in holding Icarus, to find Chloe with Sabrina tucked in one arm, and a burp cloth containing bloody milk vomit in the other.

"Something's not right," she said.

Malcolm nodded and took a moment to process the sight before him. He pointed at Chloe's chest with her boob still out and said, "your nipple is bleeding."

She felt a wave of relief wash over her as she made the connection that the blood in the milk was hers, not Sabrina's.

As Malcolm came up to her though, he noticed Icarus beginning to squirm and grunt and twist in his arms, sniffling towards Chloe.

"Pass him to me," Chloe said.

She lay Sabrina gently in her lap and took Icarus, swapping out with Malcolm. Before she knew what was happening, Icarus latched on to the bleeding nipple and began to drink like a demon possessed.

Chloe nearly cried out of relief, but Malcolm could tell from the look on her face that Icarus' feeding was painful. When he was done feeding he leaned back with the reddish pink milk blood dribbling out of his mouth. Chloe's boob had turned bruise purple around her nipple, with shades of dark blue and red streaked through her blood vessels brought to the surface of her skin.

Around the nipple Icarus had punctured four holes with his fangs, two upper, two lower, which dribbled a little blood before drying up.

Icarus fell asleep in her arms and Chloe let out a heavy sigh, glad that her precious child had had a decent feed. She hoped that he wouldn't want to feed off her blood-milk forever.

VIII

Chloe was cleaning up the excess blood from her boob with a baby wipe when the doorbell rang.

A bolt of panic struck through them and Malcolm instinctively swapped Icarus from Chloe's arms to his and slid Sabrina gently into her lap. He took Icarus, still fast asleep, into the bathroom and turned on the heat lamps.

He set a blanket down in the bathtub and placed Icarus upon it and whispered, "shh," before retreating into the lounge room to witness Chloe inviting the child health nurse into their home.

The nurse glared at Malcolm before taking Sabrina from Chloe's arms. "She should be on bed rest after the operation, Malcolm," she balanced the baby and her bag over to the coffee table and dropped her belongings off. "She certainly shouldn't be answering the door, least of all, carrying the baby to do so."

"Oh... Yes," Malcolm replied. "Of course." He felt his blood pressure rising at the sound of her attitude, especially after the midwives at the hospital had treated his wife with such apathy. He took a deep breath and silently wished that she would be in and out before Icarus could make a sound.

Malcolm took Sabrina from the nurse while she set up her scales to weigh the baby.

"This was a bit of a surprise visit," he said. "I thought we wouldn't get a house visit for a couple of weeks."

The nurse turned to him with a plastic smile on her face. "Well, usually that would be the case, but the hospital was concerned with your abrupt departure, they felt the need to check up on your baby, and wife, much sooner."

Chloe popped one of her pain management pills and sat down in the rocking chair, visibly exhausted. "I'm fine," she said, with a tone of annoyance in her voice.

The nurse undressed Sabrina, who began to protest and scream as she was placed on the scales.

Malcolm and Chloe were split in two minds whether the screams were good or bad. The good being that they would mask Icarus' cries should he start. The bad being that her cries could set him off in distress.

When the nurse was satisfied with Sabrina's health and the baby was dressed back up, she passed her still crying back to Malcolm and turned to Chloe.

"I'm fine," Chloe repeated firmly, hoping the nurse wouldn't be nearly as invasive as the midwives in the hospital.

All she wanted right now was some goddamn peace and quiet. The nurse's presence flared up Chloe's frustrations which were already so fresh from the hospital.

"How is the breastfeeding going?" the nurse asked.

"Good, good," she replied.

"You know, some mothers struggle with it from time to time, fussy babies, hormones throwing everything out of balance, and a lot of women give up and go to formula, but they forget just how important breastmilk is," the nurse said.

"I'm doing fine. Don't worry," Chloe said.

"Because you may be doing fine now," the nurse continued, "but when you do hit those problem feeding periods, it's important to remember not to give up."

"I know," Chloe said, making a mental note to disregard everything the nurse had just said. Formula was sounding like a better and better idea for Sabrina by the moment. "Stick with the breastfeeding. Got it."

"Right," the nurse said, noting the attitude. "And how are you coping, you know... Mentally? Any concerns of postnatal depression?"

Chloe thought of the first few nights in the hospital, her first moments at home, how she had never felt so hopeless, how she just couldn't comprehend a positive direction in her life beyond this point. "No, I've been settling in well, I think. The scar's a bit sore, but that's normal, that's about it," she said. Her thoughts shifted to the warm glow of Icarus in her arms, and how she couldn't wait to cuddle him the moment the nurse was out of the house.

"Good to hear," the nurse said. "Now, let's have a quick look at that scar and see how it's doing." She reached right in to Chloe's personal space and pulled her shirt up and the waistline of her pants down. A moment later, she was satisfied. "If you do notice anything strange, don't hesitate to call the hospital or pop in for a visit. For you or the baby." She flashed a hollow smile, collected her things, and left.

Chloe let out a heavy sigh and took Sabrina back in her arms. Malcolm went to check on Icarus, who was fast asleep in the bright, warm bathroom.

IX

"Shit! I'm going to be late for work," Malcolm said, ripping through his chest of drawers for a clean uniform.

"I wish you didn't have to go back to work already," Chloe said. "I don't know how I'm going to cope without you."

Malcolm paused for a moment and said, "I know, I know... But we need this money if we're going to be able to raise two children without going broke."

He pulled his red and white Mickey's shirt out and pulled it on over a white singlet. He wore neat black pants and grabbed a rubber Donald Duck mask which would fit snug over his head and cause him to sweat like a sauna.

"I can't afford to lose this job," he said, kissing Chloe on her forehead. "Call my mum for help."

"What about Icarus?" she replied. "What do we tell her? What do we tell people about him?"

"Tell my mum whatever you want, she'll love him regardless," he said. "We'll figure out the rest later, I promise."

Chloe sighed and felt like she was straight back in the hospital again, hopeless and alone. "I love you," she said as Malcolm disappeared out the door.

"I love you too," he replied. "I'll bring home dinner," and he hopped in his car and drove off.

Big Pete stood in the Mickey's parking lot smoking a cigarette through his mask and watched Malcolm park up in his usual space. He dropped the remainder of his cigarette and ground it into the asphalt before approaching the car.

Malcolm pulled his Donald Duck mask on and went to open his car door to find Pete blocking the way.

The big man leaned in on his window and growled, "you're late" in a rasping Tom Waits voice.

"Jesus Christ, Pete," Malcolm said. "Can't you give me a moment to get out of my damn car? I've just had three days off for the birth of my child, cut me a damn break."

"Okay, okay." Pete took a step back. "Congratulations," he said.

Malcolm could sense the lack of sincerity in his voice.

"Just wanted to let you know that Mickey's looking for you," Pete said. He started walking back to the restaurant.

"Shit," Malcolm said under his breath. He locked his car and followed Pete inside.

Mickey stood just inside the entrance and watched Malcolm walk in late. She pointed to her oversized cartoon watch and shook her head." Come with me," Mickey said in a stern but squeaky voice.

She was short as a child but she was of a strong, heavy build and she spoke with a thick Boston accent. Mickey was the boss of this restaurant and her authority went unquestioned.

Malcolm followed Mickey through the dining area off through a door labeled STAFF ONLY and she invited him to take a seat in her office.

"Donald, Donald, Donald," she squeaked. "Late again. Fifteen minutes. We're trying to run a business here, Donald, and this will not do."

Malcolm was no small man, but Mickey had a way with words and tone that really made him feel smaller. "I'm sorry," he mumbled. "My wife has just had her child, we're still adjusting at home."

At Mickey's the staff discarded their names and identities in favour of a cartoon likeness, they adopted these characters for the diners, but Malcolm didn't know Mickey's real name, or even what she looked like under the mask.

"Donald, we're trying to run a business here," she repeated. "You've got to separate your home family from your work family, okay?"

Malcolm nodded, "okay." He hadn't even started his shift and already it was becoming hot and sweaty and uncomfortable under the mask. It was going to be a long day at the restaurant.

"Now, I'm going to let this slide this one time, Donald, one time only," she said.

"Thank you," he replied.

"Do it again and you'll be on garbage duty for a month. A second time and you'll be handing back your face."

Malcolm was unsettled by the threat of Mickey's words coming from the big beaming face of the adorable cartoon mouse. He felt a burning embarrassment prickling through his neck and up over his face. Normally he wouldn't let others speak to him this way, but he needed this job.

"Yes boss," he said. He wanted to rip his mask off and splash his face with water, but he instead stood up to get stuck into work.

"By the way," Mickey said, "congratulations on the child. I'm happy for you."

Malcolm nodded his thanks but knew that she too was scathingly insincere.

X

Chloe took up Malcolm's suggestion to invite his mother over. Chloe knew that she would have been bursting to meet Sabrina, and felt that Malcolm's intuition would be right in that she would be equally thrilled to meet Icarus. She would love him horns and all.

Compare her to Chloe's family, none of whom she spoke with any longer. Not since her wedding, which they attended out of obligation, which they were invited to out of obligation. When they didn't approve of Chloe's black husband when he was just a boyfriend, she felt like they would all have heart attacks if they knew she was having an interracial baby with the man she loved. She felt no great loss there, only loneliness.

Chloe heard the car pull up and she felt a tightening in her chest, a rush of excitement and nervous anticipation. She held Sabrina in her arms while Icarus lay sleeping in the pram getting full sunlight from the window. His skin seemed to drink up the light and radiate a beautiful warm white glow.

Chloe opened the front door after Janet gave a short knock. Janet stepped in carrying bags of gifts and nappies and the like. She put them down just inside the door and gave Chloe and Sabrina a warm, gentle hug.

"It's so good to see you," Janet said. "Malcolm mentioned you've been having a tough time."

Chloe sighed, but smiled with relief to have Janet in good company. "Yeah, we're just trying to hold it together," she said. "And we've got a little surprise for you. Surprised the hell out of me too."

"No..." Janet said, not taking her eyes off Sabrina, brushing her hand gently across the baby's soft head. "What's the surprise?"

As if on cue, Icarus began to stir and make soft crying noises.

"There's someone else I'd like you to meet," Chloe said, walking her over towards the window and crying sounds.

When they approached the pram Janet froze, speechless, gazing at the little horned baby with confusion and a little hesitation, taking her time to process this 'surprise' of Chloe's.

"This is Icarus," Chloe said. "He... Um... He fell into our back yard on our first night home."

Janet's mind was working hard to process the unexpected child she was staring at and the words Chloe was saying. "Icarus, huh?" she said.

Chloe nodded.

"He's beautiful," Janet said. "Can I hold him?"

"Of course," Chloe said. "He's as much your grandchild as Sabrina is."

Janet leaned in and picked him up, noticing his horns for the first time. She held him to her chest.

"He sure is warm," Janet said. "Where did you say he came from?"

"He... Crash landed in our back yard," Chloe said. "Check out the crater in the back yard. I think he's some sort of alien vampire baby."

"Weird," Janet said. "That would explain his horns." She went to the back door to check out the crater and Icarus began to scream.

"He's got little fangs, too," Chloe said as Sabrina started to cry too.

"I see them!" Janet said, and hugged Icarus tight to her chest, rocking and shushing him for comfort, to which he only screamed louder. "It's okay, it's okay," she said to him in a soft and soothing voice.

He kicked and squirmed frantically in her arms and only screamed louder. According to him it was not okay.

Chloe managed to keep Sabrina from completely losing it, but Janet saw on her face that those cries combined were breaking her heart and that she would do anything, absolutely anything, to make them stop.

They went outside into the warm sun and Icarus eased his cries up a little. Janet lifted him from her chest and wiped his little tears from his scrunched up face, only for him to scream even harder, when she noticed that his skin seemed to be breaking out into some sort of purple rash.

"Just lay him down on the grass for a moment," Chloe said, speaking loud and clear to carry her voice over the cries. "He'll like that."

Janet didn't question her thought process and followed mother's orders, to find that the warm little baby stopped crying immediately and wriggled playfully in the sun.

"Poor thing," Janet said. "That rash looks horrible."

As soon as the words were out of her mouth, the marbled colours on Icarus' flesh began to ripple and shrink before her eyes, and in another moment they were gone completely. He was back to being a normal, happy, healthy baby, glowing in the golden light, being positively radiant.

"Yeah, he doesn't much like being held by Malcolm, either," Chloe said. "He loves the sun. Can't sleep at night without the heat lamps on in the bathroom, our power bills are going to kill us. This is going to sound real weird, but I think he's allergic to dark skin, and allergic to the darkness in general."

Janet stared at the magical baby a moment longer, trying to process Chloe's theory. "Huh," was all she said.

"Here," Chloe said, handing Sabrina over to Janet. "At least this one will love your cuddles."

Finally, with Icarus settled, Sabrina was able to calm down a bit, and Chloe and Janet could shift their focus to the crater in which they found Icarus.

"Well, that's just about the strangest thing I've ever seen," Janet said, walking up to the hole still half-filled with water.

"Yeah, I don't really understand it either," Chloe said. "I just know that when I held him for the first time that he had to be a permanent part of our family."

XI

Icarus began to cry again, and Chloe knew the baby was hungry. She had a variety of raw and cooked meats in the fridge she planned on trying to feed him. She pulled containers from the fridge and peeled the lids off carefully one-handed and lifted a strip of raw bacon up to Icarus.

"What are you doing?" Janet asked.

"He doesn't drink milk," Chloe replied, "we're trying to figure out what he eats."

Icarus swatted at the bacon playfully, but showed no interest in consuming it.

"He... Uh, he suckled blood from my breast earlier," Chloe admitted.

"So he's kind of like a cannibal child then, huh?" Janet said.

"More like a vampire, I think. Technically. I don't know," Chloe said. She held a strip of cooked chicken up to Icarus, who promptly turned his head away.

She tried a strip of raw steak and he sniffed eagerly and snapped at it like a turtle. A little blood dripped from the meat, and he pulled it to his face and began suckling away at it.

"I think we've found our winner," Chloe said.

"I think I feel a little sick," Janet said at the sight of the infant sucking and tearing at the raw meat.

Chloe sighed with relief and picked up a fresh strip of meat as he let his current strip fall to the floor. "I was so worried that he would have to keep feeding off me until I had nothing left to give."

Once Icarus was done feeding, Chloe's eyes welled up and tears flowed down her cheeks.

"What's wrong?" Janet asked.

"Nothing," Chloe replied, a smile on her face. "Nothing at all."

Icarus was feeding and sleeping in his own strange ways, but overall he was happy and healthy. As for Sabrina... Chloe and Malcolm could figure out her patterns and behaviours in time too. Everything was going to be okay, she felt. Tears of joy continued to pour down her face, and in that moment she didn't mind that she was beyond starving and beyond tired, not to mention that Sabrina had only just begun screaming at the top of her lungs for her next feed.

Janet stared at Chloe with a little apprehension, but she felt the love that was clicking into place for this family which was built truly like no other. She passed Sabrina off to her mother to suckle at her purple breast, and took Icarus quickly to the pram, careful not to scar his flesh too much from her skin. She didn't understand it, but she felt what Chloe felt, and her own eyes welled up with tears of pride, for how beautiful her grandchildren were, and how well her daughter-in-law had adapted to the truly unique situation she had found herself in.

XII

Malcolm got very little sleep that night. Sabrina cried and cried and nothing would keep her settled from feeding to sleeping to feeding to sleeping and on and on. And Icarus, born of light and with the taste of flesh, was demanding an abundance of both, a supply which Malcolm and Chloe couldn't consistently provide. The cost of raw, bloody meat for this child would send them broke long before their dreaded power bill.

Before Malcolm knew what was going on, he was pulling on his work uniform and grabbing his rubber mask and hopping into his car, pulling out into the street by the grey of the pre-dawn light.

He pulled into the Mickey's parking lot a full half-hour before his shift started, as a sign of good faith to his boss that his commitment to his work would not fall sacrifice to his commitment to his family.

The bills needed to be paid. The bills would always need to be paid. It became his mantra, and each time he repeated it out loud or in his mind he gained another wrinkle on his skin and/or another gray hair.

Pete was again standing in the parking lot, smoking his cigarette and watching as Malcolm got out of his car and pulled on his Donald mask. This time around, however, he said nothing. Only watching with his eyes peeping through the mask, a silent judgment from car door to restaurant door.

Inside, the chairs were overturned on the tables from the night before, the radio and the air conditioning hadn't yet been turned on for the day, so there was this calm quiet about the place which was almost surreal.

Then a door swung open and Mickey emerged from her office. "Donald," she called across the restaurant, "come, let's have another chat in my office."

Malcolm felt his chest tighten and his heart beat harder and faster. His feet felt like they had instantaneously filled with lead. Mickey's office was sacred grounds. It was always closed either occupied by Mickey herself, or kept under lock and key, or else it was for bringing about bad news.

"Take a seat," Mickey said, while she remained standing, hovering behind her desk like she was too busy for a full meeting. This wouldn't take long.

Like an obedient dog, he sat.

"I thought about our conversation yesterday," she said, shuffling items around on her desk before looking up at Malcolm. "As the manager of this franchise, I can't have the other employees thinking of me as being too soft or lenient. It's important for them to understand their role in the food chain. Things have to run perfectly or else it will quickly fall into chaos and ruin."

Malcolm felt a pit of dread growing in his stomach. "What are you getting at, Mickey?"

"It's been a good three and a half years working with you, it really has," she said.

Beneath his mask Malcolm's face grew pale. He was just waiting for the words to fall from her mouth.

She had her palms down on the table, leaning ominously over him. "I appreciate you coming in early today, it really takes the pressure off having to do this on the clock."

Any moment now, he thought.

"We're going to have to let you go."

In that instant Malcolm felt like his head, his whole body had been submerged in ice cold water. The world around him blurred and fell into an unfathomable silence.

Before he knew what was going on he came up from the ice water with a rush of adrenaline and he had his hands wrapped around Mickey's neck, wringing her throat tighter and tighter. She gasped and thrashed her arms and kicked and twisted but Malcolm held his grip firm.

He couldn't see her face under the mask but imagined it turning red then purple then blue.

He felt his fingers pressing in on her throat, collapsing, collapsing, collapsing. Like her words had collapsed his future, his children's futures.

"Donald," she said, in a clear and unchoked voice. "Donald, you have to leave."

He knew he didn't have it in him to act on his thoughts and feelings. The rage was real, so very real, and he would have loved to choke that heartless monster to death.

Instead, he sat there in stunned silence, barely even registering her words. Tears formed rivers down his face as he thought about how he would break the news to his wife.

"How dare you," he said.

"There's the door," she gestured casually towards the exit.

"How dare you," he repeated, standing up. "This aint right, Mickey."

She shrugged and pointed to the door again.

He stormed out and cleared his locker out into a

packing box and stuffed a few cartoon masks in with them for good measure.

In the car park Pete was still enjoying his morning smoke break before work started.

"Where are you off to?" he rasped.

"Get bent, Pete," Malcolm replied.

He tore off his mask and wiped the tears from his face before getting back into his car and tearing out of the Mickey's parking lot for the last time.

He drove around aimlessly for a short while, playing out a scenario in his head where he stayed out all day and pretended to Chloe that he was at work, but the guilt of leaving her at home with the babies ate away at him and he had seen enough sitcoms with this scenario to know it was not a good idea to play out.

PART TWO:
EVERYTHING IS FINE

XIII

Chloe heard a car pull up into the driveway. Her heart skipped a beat as she wondered if anyone had noticed Icarus landing in her backyard or whether someone had seen or said something about Icarus and now these strangers were here to take her alien vampire baby away. Was it child protection services? CIA? FBI? TSA? NRA? NASA?

Had the child health nurse seen anything that led her to file a report? Had Malcolm's mother actually been repulsed and scared of her bloodthirsty child? She tried to shake such thoughts from her head but in the moment it consumed her completely.

She clutched Icarus in her arms for dear life and searched frantically for an escape plan should she need to run or hide.

Frozen in the moment she heard the car door slam shut and heavy footsteps crunching along the path to the door. She waited apprehensively for a knock which never came.

A jingle of keys.

A turn of the lock.

There standing in the doorway, her husband, Malcolm. She could see where tears had streamed down his face and dried, and now he wore a scowl.

She gave an exhaustive sigh and went over to him and gave him a tight side-hug.

"Malcolm, my love, what are you doing home so early?" she asked.

He collapsed into the couch and told her, "Mickey's let me go."

"They what?" Chloe processed his words and said, "they can't."

"They can," Malcolm replied.

"They didn't," she said.

"They did," he said.

"How? Why? What happened?" she now paced the room in front of Malcolm, clutching Icarus tighter than she meant to. He grizzled and from the bedroom Sabrina woke up and cried out.

Chloe and Malcolm ignored the noise of their children.

"I was late yesterday and they told me they'd give me a warning. Today they changed their mind," Malcolm said.

"That's bullshit," Chloe said. "How are we going to feed the kids? How are we meant to pay the bills? I'll drive down there myself if I have to. I'll demand they give your job back straight away."

"It doesn't work like that, my love," Malcolm said. "I'll just... I'll just have to look for another job."

"What are we supposed to do until then?" Chloe said.

"I don't know," Malcolm said. He got up and pulled a beer from the fridge. He fell back into the couch again and cracked it open. "I don't know what we're going to do."

XIV

Malcolm had scoured the city for job openings. There were jobs seeking juniors for casual work. There were jobs seeking twenty to thirty year olds with fifteen years of specialist experience and a six year masters degree. There were temporary jobs available offering peanuts for long days, long nights on end with no commitment to a permanent position.

Malcolm was too old or too inexperienced or overqualified and nothing provided nearly enough money or security for him to support his family of four.

"We'll just have to sell the home and pay off the mortgage and live in our car," Malcolm joked to Chloe as he grabbed the last beer out of the fridge. "Or we could default on the mortgage and squat in our own home until we get forced out."

Chloe had Sabrina breastfeeding tucked around one arm and with her free hand she fed Icarus the last of the meat they had in the house.

"Could you ask your mother to take us in?" Chloe asked.

Malcolm finished a sip of his beer then shook his head. "Haven't you been to her new place yet? It's a one bedroom unit. We'd have to crash on the couch and floor. There's no space for the kids. We could maybe do a couple of nights there, but nothing long term."

"Well, we have to do something," Chloe said as Icarus finished off the meat and proceeded to hungry-cry at her. "Icarus is eating way more meat than we can possibly afford. We're going to be out on the street before we know it, dumpster diving for food, praying that we'll come across a winning lottery ticket someone accidentally threw away."

Malcolm's eyes met Chloe's, lighting up with hope. "You've just given me a brilliant idea," he said, pulling himself off the couch and kissing his wife on the forehead. He picked up Icarus and cradled the disgruntled baby in his arms.

XV

Malcolm had Icarus crudely strapped into the only baby seat in the car, wrapped in a heated jacket which was made for adults and with a star-shaped night light sitting loosely on top.

It was past midnight and he left Chloe and Sabrina sleeping peacefully for what felt like the first time since they became a family of four.

Malcolm pulled into the Mickey's parking lot and drove his car around the back. He thought about breaking in through the back entrance and loading up with groceries for his family to sort them out for the next month, but he couldn't bring himself to take that risk.

Instead he left his sleeping child to rest and lifted the lid to the dumpster, unleashing a fresh hell of unpleasant smells wafting straight into his face.

He pulled one of his stolen masks from work over his head (Pluto the dog) and climbed into the festering garbage. With his garden gloves on and a small torch light sticking out of his shirt pocket he shifted the bags of uneaten food and cooking scraps off to the side, sifting through the bags for the gold he knew was buried in there.

He coughed and choked, leaning out of the lid and lifting his mask to take a few gasps of fresh night air and check on the baby in his car. He could hear Icarus grizzling in his seat and wiggling around in the pile of jacket.

He imagined Icarus getting tangled in it and ending up face-down, suffocating on the material. He would have to be quick this time. Not that he wanted to linger around very long anyway, just in case a patrol car came driving past and decided to check him out.

After a frantic few minutes of digging he grabbed a trash bag which felt colder than the rest and he knew he had found what he was looking for. He tugged the plastic, splitting it apart to check that his intuition was right.

He sifted through the bag, nothing but cold meat which had just expired and thrown out at the end of the night. He lifted it over the lid and dropped it on the ground before climbing out himself.

He felt sweaty from crawling through the dumpster and wearing the rubber Pluto mask, and he pulled it off to take some fresh air. He looked around to find that there was no one else around. He scooped up the meat sack and put it in the boot of his car, checked on Icarus squirming in the back seat, and drove home.

He would sleep in the morning while Chloe looked after the babies.

XVI

Malcolm woke up to a baby screaming. Sabrina. He knew the tone of her screams well and would surely remember them long after they had caused him to lose his hearing.

Chloe stumbled into the bedroom with a look of complete hopelessness about her.

"She won't stop screaming," she said. "I've tried everything. I don't know what's wrong."

Malcolm groggily lifted his head from his pillow as his mind started to process what was going on around him. Chloe placed Sabrina screaming and squirming down in the middle of the bed.

"I've got to feed Icarus," she said. "You take care of this one."

Then she left the room, closing the door behind her. Malcolm scooped Sabrina gently up and gave her a pacifier from his bedside table. Her mouth closed around it and she moaned and suckled and her cries died down and then she was asleep in his arms.

He carried her out of the bedroom and sat down in his chair, watching Chloe from the lounge room as she fed Icarus in the kitchen.

It had only been days but since he started feeding he was already twice Sabrina's size and sitting up on his own, reaching for the raw meat and ripping into it with his razor sharp teeth. He ate so much and so ravenously, yet he wasn't a fat child. He seemed to be feeding proportionately to his growth patterns. And yet when he did feed his stomach grew out big and round like he had swallowed a giant marble or a very tiny planet.

"I'm going to need to get more meat soon, yeah?" Malcolm said.

"Yeah, this will only last a couple of days, I think," Chloe said. "And we've still got to feed ourselves somehow."

"I can ask my mother to prepare some meals for us," he said.

Chloe let Icarus suckle the blood and juices from her fingers, strangely confident that he wouldn't consume his mother's flesh. "You can get another job for a start."

"There's fucking nothing out there," he snapped.

Sabrina flinched at the volume of his voice, and he rocked her gently and shushed her back down. He whispered, "there's fucking nothing out there, I've been looking constantly."

"Well you've got to look harder. We can't rely on your mother's charity all the time. We can't rely on your dumpster diving to feed the family." Chloe lowered the volume of her voice too and lifted Icarus up to her shoulder.

"I'm trying, okay?" he said. "It's hard enough raising one baby, let alone two, let alone all the other shit we've got to deal with now. Not to mention that Icarus is a god damn giant. What are we going to do, we can't keep up with him going at this rate."

"My back is killing me," Chloe said, clearly struggling to carry her child around.

She put him down on a mat on the floor and he immediately rolled over and crawled his way over to the coffee table to put the tv remote in his mouth.

She rushed forward to stop him, only to get a response of hysteric cries that cuddles or toys with distracting noises couldn't pacify.

"I'm at my wit's end, I really am," Chloe picked Icarus back up. "Every day. I don't know how we can survive like this."

She struggled to focus, to think while Icarus was crying. It was like an interference signal in her brain.

Malcolm was talking back to her, although she couldn't focus enough to hear him, let alone process the words. She could assume he was agreeing with her. The stress was getting to both of them, and it was highly likely that he was struggling to focus and think with all this screaming going on too.

Sabrina was now wide awake and looking ready to burst into tears again, when Malcolm stood up and placed her down on the mat where she lay turtling helplessly for a moment, giving Malcolm the free arms to take Icarus and carry him to the bathroom.

The heat lamps clicked on and the exhaust fan started up and in the warm glow of the bathroom lights, Icarus' cries lost their edge and he didn't fight when Malcolm put him down in the makeshift cot in the bathtub and left him to cry it out a minute.

Malcolm came back to Chloe cuddling a now happy Sabrina. He gave her a side-hug and said, "sit down, my love, I'll make you a coffee."

In the kitchen he took out two mugs and took two deep breaths and closed his eyes a moment and tried to collect himself before returning to Chloe.

He felt like a plate of jelly which under the circumstances had to become a rock.

XVII

The following day he spent searching for jobs again. Circling ads and calling places and preparing copies of his resumé, knowing that none of the jobs he was applying for would pay enough for him to support his family, and even if he were able to stack three or four of these jobs around each other, he would still be stretching it, still coming up short.

And he was adding this to the thought that none of these jobs were really secure, as he thought of the ease with which Mickey fired him in the first place, his prospects were a terrifying thing.

These were the thoughts flooding his mind whenever he wasn't dealing with a tired or hungry or otherwise upset baby. Or a tired and hungry and upset wife.

When he found himself with a moment's clear thought he trailed away from the bleak job prospects and instead thought about his next dumpster dive. He knew hitting Mickey's again wouldn't provide much, and wouldn't offer the variety that he would need to feed anyone but his vampire child. He thought of the Agrabah Megamart just down the road from Mickeys which would probably provide a bountiful harvest.

He thought of what clothes he would wear that were nice and dark and hard to see in the dead of night. He also thought of leaving his poor wife in the night to wake up and deal with the feeds of needy screaming babies in his absence, one setting off the other, the fatigue compounding and the ability to remain composed in the face of chaos and terror just slipping through her fingers like water.

He wanted to bring both kids sleeping peacefully in the car, and he wanted to feed a ravenous Icarus straight from the dumpster, to fill up on what he couldn't fit in the car. And yet their car still only had one child seat, and unless he found one in a warped and wrecked car on the side of the road, he knew they wouldn't be getting one any time soon. Not to mention that bringing either child on the dumpster dive was a greater risk to get caught. And then what? And then how could he provide for his family even the most meager of supplies to get them through the next few days.

Malcolm tried to search for more jobs again the next day, but Sabrina was getting so worked up and she wasn't feeding properly or sleeping properly and Chloe couldn't quite tell if she had a temperature or if she was just warm because of all the screaming.

Chloe took the car to get out of the house and catch a breather and left Malcolm to try to bring the babies under control. He knew she needed that break to mentally pull herself back together, but his mind couldn't help wandering to the fuel she was using driving off to who knows where.

He guessed she would drive off up into the hills to visit her friend, Aurora, to chew her ear off while Icarus chewed at Malcolm's ear because he had devoured the last of the meat. Malcolm hoped that if she had gone to see Aurora, that at least she was getting a decent feed there and hopefully a bit of a rest and if he was lucky that maybe she would bring home a dish of some delicious homecooked meal he could also enjoy.

With Icarus put down to rest in the sun by the lounge room window, Malcolm took to dealing with Sabrina. She was still screaming relentlessly on and off, and she had already been pumped full of syringes of child medicine to help calm her for pain or gut discomfort or whatever else he could practically think of without overdosing her on all the stuff. He ripped open the tin of formula Chloe had bought before Sabrina's birth on the off-chance that breastfeeding didn't go to plan, and he made up a fresh bottle praying that she would take it and give him some peace before he too broke down and had to leave the babies temporarily to fend for themselves.

As he sat down on the lounge chair with Sabrina cradled in his arms, squirming and screaming and displaying far more strength than she should have been able, he felt a wave of relief as she began to suckle at the bottle like it was no big deal all along and that she was totally satisfied with her lot in life in this moment.

XVIII

When Chloe returned home she was somewhat more composed, yet still reluctant to let Malcolm go dumpster diving in the night. She had visited Aurora like Malcolm had guessed, and brought home a meatloaf and potato bake for them to eat, along with a small amount of frozen meat for Icarus.

After another big feed, Icarus fell into a deep sleep in the bathroom tub, while Sabrina woke in the middle of the night, squirming and crying. At the first cries Chloe's milk started leaking and she reluctantly sat up in bed, clearly bitter at the constant broken sleep that was putting so much stress on both her body and her mind.

"I can make her a bottle if you'd like," Malcolm said as he lifted Sabrina from her bassinet.

Chloe grunted a "yeah, fine," before sliding back down and rolling over to return to sleep.

Malcolm carried Sabrina out of the bedroom, holding his breath as he walked past the bathroom, tiptoeing quickly, listening out to notice if her cries would wake the other one.

It did not.

He made the bottle and she drank ravenously, falling back to sleep as she fed in his arms. He sat in the lounge chair and let her settle on his shoulder before bringing her back to bed.

Sabrina was fast asleep. Chloe was fast asleep. Malcolm was pretty sure Icarus was fast asleep too. He checked the time on his phone before pulling on his jeans and a black hoodie. He slipped his boots on in the hall and grabbed the keys off the counter. His masks and gloves were in the car ready for his next dumpster dive.

He could feel the excitement in his bones, the thought of providing for his family, sneaking around in secret and stealing from the system, Malcolm couldn't deny that it gave him a rush.

Before he knew it he was parked out the back of the Agrabah Megamart. Lights off, engine off, mask and gloves on, torch in hand, ready to go.

He clicked his torch on and the brick wall of the back of the building revealed a graffiti desert mural with a Cave of Wonders surrounding the dumpster. Bright red letters were sketched across the dumpster itself, reading, "who disturbs my slumber?"

Malcolm knew he couldn't waste any time on this dumpster dive, so he took a deep breath and lifted the lid and dug in. Unlike Mickey's, the Agrabah Megamart held a far wider variety of discarded goods. Not only was there a larger jackpot of raw meats, but also misshapen and slightly over-ripe fruits and vegetables starting to wilt. Cereal boxes with holes in the corner, the bags still intact, piles and piles of perfectly good product with damaged packaging.

Malcolm wished he had a trailer so he could load up and haul away this perfectly good waste. Some bags were actual garbage but few were damaged beyond use or rotten or otherwise expired to the point of no return. He grabbed a couple of loaves of bread and some dented tins of tuna and he formed an unfeasably large pile outside the dumpster to scoop up into his car when he called it quits.

It was thrilling, yet a little disheartening, knowing that companies like Agrabah would rather all this good product to go to waste than potentially feed and care for dozens of families like his, or hundreds of street rats living in cardboard tents every night. Malcolm felt vomit rising in his throat which he believed wasn't related to his being in the dumpster.

He kept digging for more, for better, for jackpot. Anything he could bring home for Sabrina or Icarus or Chloe to prove his time was well invested. Some pacifiers or bottles or if he struck gold, some tins of formula.

The time seemed to sink inside the dumpster like quicksand and by the time Malcolm was scraping at the bottom he was sucked back into the real world by some gunshots no more than a couple of blocks away, followed by a nearby baby crying.

He thought of what would happen if he were caught red-handed, if the risk would have been worth it then. He peeked out of the dumpster and sighed upon noticing the back parking lot of the Agrabah Megamart was still empty and the only sound punctuating the cold night air was the crying baby coming from a nearby property.

Malcolm loaded up his goods and made for home as quick and stealthy as he could, hoping that his wife and two babies were still all fast asleep. He was playing a fool's game, sneaking out without her permission, and of course Chloe was awake and giving Sabrina a bottle feed, sending Malcolm piercing silent daggers as he came through the door with an armload of garbage.

XIX

"How could you have left us like that?" Chloe said, glaring at Malcolm with his haul, the pride of his successful dive sliding from the smile on his face. "I can't believe you would be so reckless."

Malcolm let the garbage drop to the floor, bread squishing a little more than it already had been. "I don't exactly have a lot to work with. The job market isn't really seeking employees right now. And the ones that are, they sure aren't calling on me." He fished into his garbage bag and pulled out a green apple, biting into it with a sharp crunch, an acidic tang bursting in his mouth.

"You know we can't live like this," Chloe said. "We've got bills to pay soon. We've got a mortgage. You can't show up to job interviews smelling like garbage and running on no sleep. Not to mention that I need you here to help with the babies too."

I know, my love, but we've got to be able to have something we can feed this family. And a lot of this stuff is really good. It's just going to waste otherwise." Malcolm pulled a crumpled bag of chips out of his garbage bag and threw them onto Chloe's lap. "See? It's just a bit crushed is all."

Chloe's stomach grumbled. She hadn't eaten since yesterday afternoon and all the running around taking care of the babies, losing sleep, Sabrina draining the nutrients in her body through her milk, and now she had succumbed to formula over breastmilk these past couple of feeds, she felt drained, unfulfilled, defeated. She passed Sabrina over to Malcolm and tore into the chips. She had gone to the pantry countless times since Malcolm lost his job, and each time it looked more and more bleak.

"What if you get caught?" Chloe asked through a mouthful of chips.

Before he could respond Icarus let out a piercing scream from the bathroom.

"This isn't over," Chloe said. "You get some meat ready for his feed, okay?"

Malcolm nodded and carried Sabrina into the kitchen while Chloe went to fetch Icarus.

She approached the bathroom door and gave a gasp as she noticed there was no light seeping through the crack at the bottom. The screams grew louder and more urgent and she ripped open the door to find the heat lamps had blown and that the darkness had consumed her precious fragile child.

She rushed in and reached into the tub to pick up Icarus, but he was writhing violently and thrashing his arms and legs about and gnashing his teeth like mad. He scratched her and bit at her hands unknowingly and she screamed out in pain. His claws and teeth were far sharper than a child's ought to be.

Malcolm rushed to check on her to find her coming out of the bathroom with a still-screaming Icarus clenched tightly in her bleeding arms. Her face was sweaty and pale although Malcolm nearly dropped Sabrina from the shock of the sight of Icarus, snaking black tendrils blossoming on his skin, forming dark purple welts in clusters all over his body. His eyes were bloodshot red with yellowed whites and his head thrown back, screaming like they had never heard before.

"Where's the meat?" Chloe yelled, knowing Malcolm had no chance of hearing. "The meat, we need to get some food in him."

Malcolm was frozen into a stupor between the sight of his wounded wife and his shrieking son. Chloe pushed past him, sticking a finger into Icarus' mouth to try soothing him. He clamped down and suckled away and his cries settled down as Chloe tried to control the pain that she was in as Icarus gnawed at her knuckles and broke the skin on her finger with ease.

She sat him on the kitchen counter and used her free hand to stuff a bit of meat in the side of his mouth, hopefully enough to allow herself to pull her finger free.

XX

Chloe's finger was shredded worse than she had thought. Icarus' sharp teeth had torn down the length of her finger, leaving a few meaty strings dangling by a little bit of flesh. Upon first noticing it she thought it would need stitches, but upon closer inspection she doubted whether stitches would even do anything to help her at this point.

Malcolm placed Sabrina in the pram and took Icarus from her and she collapsed onto the kitchen floor, shuddering in silent tears. His body was cold and clammy like a hunk of meat he had only just pulled out of the fridge.

Malcolm held Icarus tight, hoping his body heat would radiate into his child. He carried Icarus out to his car and pulled out the heated jacket and night light, wrapping Icarus up tight to keep the warmth in.

Icarus had calmed down now, but he still looked monstrously ill. The night light was glowing in his face, with his flesh looking sickly streaked purple on his pale face. By the light, his eyes looked even more yellow, with a thick gunk leaking from them like tears.

Back inside, Malcolm placed Icarus in his bundle of clothing on the floor in the lounge room, only to find his wife still sobbing and shaking in the same spot on the kitchen floor. He disappeared into the dark bathroom and came back with a first aid kit and a clean towel to wrap her in.

He wrapped her up and hugged her tight and felt damp patches forming on the towel where the blood was soaking through. He carried her into the lounge room where Icarus was looking much happier in his warm jacket wrap, and he sat Chloe down into the armchair.

There was a trail of blood dripping on the carpet where Chloe walked over, and the armchair would need a good clean too, but right now Malcolm peeled back the towel a little, unsticking it from Chloe's bloody flesh, the gashes running long and deep all over her arms. The finger which was mutilated so bad Malcolm thought there was no chance of saving it.

He got out the antiseptic wipes and ran them along the length of her wounds, causing her to wince and cry, emitting a high-pitched squeal as she tried to resist the pain. Childbirth had already put her through hell and back, and now she felt like she just couldn't get any relief.

The pain on her arms felt worse than you would expect, simply because of the mental strain of their new family circumstances, the physical toll of carrying a child, getting it cut out, and raising two babies with no idea how to do anything right. Her back and arms and legs and abdomen were constantly sore as is, the cuts now burned and she felt utterly weak and helpless.

Malcolm wrapped her arms in gauze, with the wounds starting to bleed through and stick as soon as he applied it. He mummified Chloe's arms, wrapping over and over until the bleeding was confined. Then he wrapped her finger, trying to be mindful of the shredded flesh, but knew she needed to get to a hospital soon.

He knew that Icarus likely needed to see a doctor too, but it was going to be challenging enough to bring his wife in and trying to explain all the scratch marks and the bitten finger. How he would explain a little meat-eating vampire child with a severe allergy to darkness was completely beyond him.

And then Malcolm worked himself up into a panic over how he was going to get Chloe to the hospital in the first place. They only had the one car seat at the moment and the two babies. Chloe couldn't drive herself in this condition and he couldn't leave one of the babies at home alone. He couldn't exactly run the risk of having one of the babies loose in the car either with all the maniacs which were out on the road all the time and far more noticeable since the babies came into their lives.

Malcolm gave Chloe whatever pain medication they had in the cupboard and said, "I'll have to call my mum over to watch the babies."

Chloe nodded and tried to focus on something other than the pain.

Sabrina started crying for her next feed and Malcolm felt a nasty headache brewing in his skull, the culmination of various things ripping at his attention and building pressure, demanding his attention above all else. He wanted to pop a couple of pills but they were running low and he knew he needed to save them for the time being. He got his mother on the phone on speaker and prepared the bottle, taking deep breaths to calm his nerves as his wife sat over in the next room quietly suffering, waiting for the help she desperately needed.

XXI

Janet was there as soon as they could have reasonably hoped, as painful as the wait was for Chloe, just sitting, festering in her wounds. She worried over the questions the doctors would ask, the implications drawn against Malcolm when her answers would inevitably fail to satisfy their curiosity or fill their duty of care to know that she would be safe in a household with him.

She knew they would have had to have seen some pretty horrific things over the years, but she worried all the same. She stressed over the cost of the healthcare. The bill spilling over the hundreds of dollars into the thousands just from sitting in a bed or running basic tests, performing basic medical assistance in bandaging her up in a clean and sterile manner.

She saw a future loan growing uncomfortably large to keep her fighting fit, to ensure her bank account would be ruined beyond repair for the rest of her foreseeable future, for poverty to be the only future her kids would grow up in, the failings of a model where being sick and poor is a business model of those so far ahead of her and Malcolm in life that the concepts of fair and unfair were just the snowflake on the tip of the injustice iceberg.

None of this was fair. None of this was a thing they had a single element of control over.

Chloe was seen in emergency by a nurse who stitched up what she could, bandaged the majority of cuts across her arms, and scratched her head at the mutilated finger.

Chloe mumbled some weak excuse about stray dogs, not thinking about the consequences or added cost of needing a rabies shot, but the nurse either seemed not to notice or seemed not to care. She left Chloe to stew in her panic before returning a couple of minutes later with a doctor to inspect the wound. He took one look at it and told the nurse to glue it, and then he moved on to the next patient.

There was no lengthy interrogation, no elaborate hospital stay. In another five minutes the loose strips of her finger were glued back into place and bandaged back up. In half an hour she was cleared for release with a bill that unsurprisingly would spiral them further into debt.

When Malcolm was bringing Chloe back to the car he made a joke under his breath how he should upgrade from diving in dumpsters to robbing banks.

Chloe was not amused, least of all because she was still in significant pain, considering how she denied pain medication order to keep the costs down, not that it would have affected the outcome much at all.

Either way they felt like they were watching their lives crumble around them.

XXII

They came home to Janet struggling to hold everything together. Sabrina had been demanding all of her attention with constant screaming and refusing to sleep or eat and screeched over anything that involved being put down or handled in any way whatsoever.

Janet felt somewhat capable of dealing with the crying as it wasn't her child she had to live with this time around. She had been there before and survived, although she could tell already that Sabrina was far more challenging than her kids ever were.

Then there was the monster child who she now considered with apprehension and fear after knowing what Icarus had done to his mother just this morning.

She threw meat at him to keep him satisfied, and he would grab it, turn it in his hands and suck it into his mouth, ripping the big pieces of flesh down with his razor sharp teeth.

Janet had no words to describe this child. And with the black rashes streaking over his skin, and his yellowed eyes, she was more than a little disturbed compared to her last visit when he was so much smaller and more placid and less active, less ravenous.

She could see him growing and developing in leaps and bounds, far ahead of what his age and progress should have been, but who was she to doubt a child who came from outer space to consume the mortal flesh of the land?

She still found herself while cuddling the distressed Sabrina, gazing at this other disturbing child, Icarus, with a full heart, and she knew that if she were in Chloe's position she would have held him close as he scratched the shit out of her too and let him gnaw away at her flesh if she thought it would soothe him.

Now that Chloe was back Janet was more than happy to reunite Sabrina with her parents, with Sabrina almost instantly turning into a calm and happy baby in Malcolm's arms, undermining Janet's ordeal completely.

Janet couldn't help but stare at the bandages up and down Chloe's arms and felt her own arms itching with phantom wounds as she imagined Icarus in distress and lashing out at her too.

Malcolm showed his mother the medical bill and said "I don't know how we're going to cover this."

She wrapped her arms around him and Sabrina, and she could feel the stress built up inside him. "It will be okay, Malcolm," she said. "I'll take care of this. I've got a bit of savings tucked away I was going to put towards a college fund for Sabrina, but you need it more now."

Chloe gently brushed a bandaged arm across Janet's back and said, "we can't possibly accept that gift, it's too much." At the same time she knew she couldn't refuse it either.

"Nonsense," Janet replied. "It was meant for you regardless, for your family. There's nothing I wouldn't do for you."

Chloe was tearing up and Malcolm was lost for words. "Thank you," she said. "You're an angel."

XXIII

The meat seemed to help with Icarus' healing. He ate so much and continued to grow like a monster truck, it was hard to believe he was just 'born' such a short time ago.

He needed more meat. Fresh meat. Malcolm was learning to live in a constant state of tension, finding more meat, providing Icarus with heat, and making sure he had a constant source of light. There was something carnal, something primal about this relationship.

As much as Malcolm and Chloe were dreading their next power bill, neither of them wanted to let Icarus slip into the darkness like that again.

And Janet really was their saving grace. She came over to their home every day while Chloe was healing.

Once Chloe's arms were good enough that she could pick up her children again, Janet took Malcolm out to their local Agrabah Megamart to pick up a second car seat so they could leave the house with both Sabrina and Icarus when they needed to. And to buy more meat for the flesh-hungry child.

Malcolm brought Icarus along with them to give Chloe some relief, leaving her with the 'safe' child, although Sabrina often felt like the more difficult of the two. Malcolm had Icarus in the pram with his night light and heated jacket and he covered the pram up to keep Icarus hidden from prying eyes, to hide the horns and fangs, although he knew some weirdly obsessed strangers would attempt to forcefully pry whether he liked it or not.

They walked into the megamart, greeted by a human in a blue vest and puffy off-white pants with a fez sitting delicately on his head.

"Welcome to Agrabah Megamart," the door greeter said, almost robotically.

"Good morning," Janet replied.

Malcolm smiled and nodded and pushed the pram past the employee and into the vast, sprawling discount store, themed after a Middle-Eastern bazaar reminiscent of Disney's Aladdin, and the fictional city of Agrabah.

Malcolm and Chloe, prior to having kids, and like nearly everyone else, did most of their shopping here. The aisles set up like market displays rarely changed, with only the prominent impulse-buy sections rotating with the seasons.

It didn't take long before Malcolm and Janet were deep within the maze of markets, occasionally passing employees dressed like Jafar or Jasmine or the palace guards as they restocked the market displays, every time turning to them and saying some close variant of "hi, can I help you with anything today?"

Malcolm always interjected with a "no thank you" and kept walking. He could feel this place sucking the soul from him and didn't want to stay longer than he needed to at the best of times, least of all now that he was pushing around a baby who might throw a tantrum out of hunger or fatigue or literally anything else at any time.

He steered the pram towards the car seats where they were stacked in boxes on pallets and a giant tent-like stall framed the entire display, with vibrant colours assaulting his eyes. Another reason he couldn't stand this place. With the aisle clear, Malcolm lifted the cover on the pram and let Icarus look around. Icarus loved all the bright colours, turning his head from one side of the aisle to the other, trying to look at everything at the same time.

Malcolm grabbed the cheapest car seat that looked like it would last a few years and put it in Janet's trolley. He covered the pram again and as he walked on to find the meat counter Janet put the seat back and grabbed one of the higher end ones. This place was still cheap as hell after all.

As they approached the meat section Icarus became visibly more excited, kicking his legs and flailing his arms and pulling at the restraints which held him in the pram, shaking it like crazy. Malcolm waited for someone to come check if his child was okay. He hoped his presence, an over-tired and sick-of-this-bullshit black man would ward people off from getting too close to him and his baby. There was just something about babies that pulled people in, whether you wanted to interact with them or not. He peeked in the pram to check if Icarus' hoodie was still in place covering his horns. They were.

The people working at the counter were dressed as the sultan's palace guards, using scimitars to chop meat for the fridge display and for the customers. Malcolm ordered the biggest, cheapest hunk of meat they had and slapped it in the trolley. Janet ordered a second for them.

"What else is on your shopping list?" Janet asked.

Malcolm listed off a small handful of essentials, omitting every other thing they needed, knowing his mother would insist on buying the lot and refusing to take no for an answer. Malcolm wanted more than anything to be independent, to be capable of providing for his family, but he knew he needed all the help she was willing to give. He was also growing more nervous the longer they stayed at the megamart. All the worst case scenarios unfolded in his mind.

Janet added extra things into the trolley as they went around the megamart, and Malcolm occasionally added something he had purposely left off his list, knowing that this was the time to swallow his pride and accept his mother's help. He tried not to linger in any one spot for too long, knowing the quicker they got the shopping over and done with, the sooner he could get home and relax somewhat. Or at least get a breather from the suffocating air of public spaces.

XXIV

With the extra car seat and all the groceries, it became a game of tetris to fit everything in the car along with Malcolm, Janet, Icarus, and the pram.

"Thank you," Malcolm said as they drove home.

"Don't think anything of it," Janet replied. "I just want your family to be happy and healthy."

"No, seriously, thank you. I don't know what we'd do without your help," he said.

"I couldn't live with myself if I let you struggle on your own," she said. "You'll find your feet again. It's just hard. I understand. I've been there before. You will find your way."

"Oh shit," Malcolm said, police lights flickered in his rear vision mirror and a short burst of siren penetrated the air. Icarus jerked at the sound and began screaming. Malcolm's heart leapt into his throat, all the public interactions between black folk and cops replaying in his mind.

He had been driving so carefully, he wondered what he had possibly done wrong. The thought that nothing came to mind felt even worse, being pulled over for no reason panicked him more than if he had actually been doing something wrong.

The officer walked up to the driver's window and Malcolm wound it down like a good obedient citizen. But with the screaming in the back seat he couldn't think clearly. The officer was talking to him but Icarus was drowning him out.

The officer repeated himself, "license and registration, please."

Malcolm complied, glancing at the officer's badge as he did so. It read BURNS, then he looked up at the officer's face. His stern expression did nothing to break the tension or put Malcolm at ease.

"Is everything alright, officer?" Janet said sweetly as she leaned across.

"I'll be asking the questions here," he snapped. "Maybe you could do something about shutting that mongrel up," he pointed at Icarus.

Malcolm gripped his steering wheel tighter than he meant to. He felt numb. He didn't know what else to do. He didn't know what was wrong, or what was right. He glanced at Icarus in the rearview mirror, reflected in the mirror fixed to the headrest on the back seat. He noticed his baby's horns as two lumps noticeable in the outline of the hoodie pulled up over his head. He hoped the officer wouldn't care to look, or if he did, that he wouldn't notice.

"You've got quite a full car here," Burns said, pointing at the boxed baby seat and groceries taking up the entire back seat of the car. "I was surprised you were able to see my lights through your back windshield."

"Is that an issue?" Malcolm said, instantly regretting that his tone could have been misread as hostile.

"It's an issue for emergency services trying to clear the roads to save lives, yeah," Burns said. He started writing a ticket.

"Please, just cut me a break, I didn't know," Malcolm said. Icarus continued to scream.

"Cut the excuses," Burns said. "And would one of you shut that kid up before I do it myself."

Malcolm felt his fear turn to rage. "If you're going to give me a ticket, then give me the damn ticket. But don't threaten to harm my child."

Janet got out of the front seat to collect Icarus from the back and soothe him.

"Hey hey, I didn't say you could get out of the vehicle ma'am," Burns snapped. "I'm gonna have to ask my friend here uh..." he looked to Malcolm's license in his hand. "Malcolm, step out of the vehicle and keep your hands clear where I can see them."

Malcolm noticed Burns' hand resting on his holster and his rage swung wildly back to fear, and he complied with the officer's orders. He glanced at the other cop still sitting in the vehicle, watching their every move.

Janet rocked and bounced Icarus from the other side of the car and yet he screamed louder than before.

"Shut that baby up ma'am, I'm not going to ask you again," Burns said.

"It's a baby, that's what they do," Malcolm said.

"Get down on the ground with your hands behind your head," Burns said, lifting his gun from its holster.

"What?" Malcolm said, and immediately regretted it.

"You heard me. Down. Now." He pointed the gun at Malcolm.

"This is ridiculous," Janet said.

"Stay out of it, ma'am. Or I'll arrest you too for disobeying a direct order and obstruction of justice," he said.

"What justice? This is ridiculous," she replied.

Malcolm was on the ground already, willing his mother and child to be compliant but they defied him in their own ways. Janet came around the front of the vehicle to shift Burns' focus away from her son.

"I said stay out of it," Burns said, and he raised his

gun to her and a loud bang echoed through the street.

Before they could register what had happened, Icarus had transmuted with a loud crack into a bat-shaped creature of burning light and flew lightning fast at the officer's face, hitting it with such force that it burst like a bomb, sending hot flesh scattering over Malcolm and Janet, and across Malcolm's car, the cop car, and in a wide arc across the street. The other officer stepped out of his car to watch his partner alive one moment, fall headless on the side of the road the next.

There was another loud bang and he too burst his head into pieces and fell to the ground.

A moment later, Icarus was sitting happily in Janet's arms, blood staining around his mouth. Horns fully exposed in the daylight. Malcolm looking up from his awkward position on the ground as Janet stood in shocked silence at the crime scene before them.

They looked around for any passing vehicles or people approaching on the footpath nearby, surprised and blessed that they were alone. Janet clipped Icarus back into his car seat while Malcolm dusted himself off, snatched his license and registration back, the half-written ticket, and got in the driver's seat, peeling back onto the road with the image of the headless cops burned into his mind.

PART THREE:
WHERE THERE IS LIGHT, THERE IS HOPE

XXV

"We need to leave town," Malcolm said.

Chloe looked at him with narrow eyes, noticing the blood spatter on his clothes and hair. "What happened?" she asked.

"We need to leave right now. Get as far away as we can. Let's get far away. Find a nice small town and settle down," he put Icarus down in the middle of the lounge room, blood still caked around his mouth and covering his body.

"What happened?" Chloe asked again, but Malcolm had already disappeared out the front door as Janet came in with an armful of groceries. "What happened?" she asked Janet.

Janet unloaded the groceries in the kitchen and Chloe followed. "Chloe, love, it was horrible," Janet said. "We were stopped by the police on the way home. It was turning real nasty real quick." She paused to take a deep breath and find the words to continue. "They had Malcolm on the ground, with their guns drawn."

"Holy shit," Chloe said.

"Yep," Janet continued. "Then Icarus... He... He just kind of ate them? I don't know. It happened so fast."

Malcolm came into the kitchen with more groceries and Chloe wrapped her arms around him.

"I'm so glad you're safe and sound," she said. Then she turned back to Janet and asked, "what do you mean, Icarus ate them?"

"I don't know," she replied. "One moment I was holding him in my arms, the next, he transformed into some form of wild thing and flew over to the cops. Sounded like a gunshot, then their heads exploded."

Malcolm kissed his wife on the forehead. "It's okay now. We're all safe. But we witnessed two cops die and no one will believe what happened. We can't hang around long enough for them to track us down."

Tears welled in Chloe's eyes and she nodded that she understood. This family thing was tougher than she ever imagined. Right now she felt as though the whole lot of them were all drowning.

XXVI

(Malcolm and Chloe run through all the different things holding them back. The house, the babies, the lack of money, the lack of job. They resign to the fact that they just have to wait and see.)

That night Sabrina and Icarus seemed to sleep more peacefully than they ever had before.

Chloe and Malcolm couldn't sleep at all. They put nature documentaries on the tv for background noise, but even the soothing voice of David Attenborough couldn't calm their frantic minds.

"I thought I was going to die today," Malcolm said, laying in bed and staring across the pillow at his wife.

"I don't know how we've survived as a family this long, honestly," she replied. She wrapped an arm around him.

"I keep seeing those cops with their heads missing every time I close my eyes," Malcolm said. "I don't think I'll ever be able to unsee that image."

"What are we going to do?" Chloe asked. "About Icarus? We can't just let him grow up around people, he's so dangerous."

They fell quiet for a moment. David Attenborough rambled on about migratory fish and predatory birds.

"I mean, what if he turns on one of us?" Chloe said quietly, feeling monstrous for voicing such a thought about her own child. "He's a killer. That's what he is, right? The things he's capable of..."

"He was protecting me," Malcolm replied. "I think." In truth, he wasn't quite sure.

He thought of a hypothetical scenario where he and Chloe were having a petty argument. Would Icarus intervene and attack Malcolm for yelling too loud or punching a wall or something? In an instant it felt like they were walking on eggshells around him, cautious of the potential within him, a power they knew nothing about.

"I hope you're right," Chloe said. "I still love him so much. I just don't know what to do now. Where do we go so we can raise him without fear?"

"I don't know," Malcolm replied. "But I still love him too."

"How are we going to do this?" Chloe asked. "How can we just uproot our lives and relocate out of the blue?"

Malcolm lay there in contemplation. He sighed. "I have no idea," he admitted. "We can't get a new place in a new town until I get a new job." The words tasted bitter as they fell out of his mouth. "It's a catch-22."

"And in the mean time we've still got our mortgage to deal with," Chloe said. "If we leave this place we've still got to deal with this house. We can't just sell it off at the drop of a hat and move. These things take time that we don't have."

"Do we go on an impromptu holiday and see where we end up?" Malcolm asked.

"I don't know about you, my love, but I don't have the energy to go traveling with the two babies, not knowing where we're going, how we'll manage the travel, let alone feeding and settling them day and night, pulling gas money from thin air, or winding up in another scenario where Icarus harms other people."

Malcolm sighed again. "You're right."

"We'll just have to ride it out," Chloe said. "See if anyone comes knocking. Guess we're stuck here for now."

"Guess so," Malcolm replied.

There was a moment of silence before Chloe muttered "Goodnight" and Malcolm rolled over and closed his eyes, trying to will himself to sleep but the visceral images were too fresh in his mind to allow a moment's peace.

XXVII

In the morning Malcolm took the car and left Chloe on her own with Sabrina and Icarus. He pulled up to their local Al's Toy Bar when he got a message from Chloe asking where he was and why he left without an explanation.

Instead, he paid attention to the message from his former co-worker, Big Pete, or Terry, as he was called outside his job when he left his cartoon character behind.

Terry had arrived just a few minutes earlier, ready to help Malcolm talk through any concerns he had. It was too early for a drink, but Al's Toy Bar was a 24-hour establishment and Malcolm felt that it was too early in life for his son to become a murderer, but if that could happen then he could damn well have a whiskey before breakfast.

Terry had a cola and a seat in a booth where Malcolm could get comfortable and open up. They were never unkind to each other at work, but they were never all that close outside of work either, so Terry knew it must have been quite serious for Malcolm to break down and ask for his help and his company like he did.

He got his drink from the bar and thought of the high staff turnover in bars. The bar was decorated with all sorts of Toy Story memorabilia, posters for Woody's Roundup and Buzz Lightyear's Space Command. The bartender had a space cadet outfit on and a glossed-over expression on his face.

Malcolm wondered if he could find a job opening in a place like this and earn his wages pouring drinks for sorry souls like himself all day and/or night.

He slid into the booth opposite Terry and took a sip of his drink. It burned, which felt appropriate for the circumstances he found himself in. His phone vibrated with missed phone calls and messages from Chloe wanting to know where he was, an explanation or response or anything, but all he could think about were those headless bodies.

"What's on your mind, my man?" Terry rasped in his Tom Waits voice.

Malcolm wasn't sure how to put it into words so he kept it simple and vague. "Things have just been incredibly tough lately," he said. "Everything just feels like it's sucking the life out of me. It's taken everything from me and keeps asking for more. It's just... I've got no idea what I'm doing or where I'm going. I'm scared, not just for myself. For my wife, for my family now. Whether I like it or not, we're stuck here together."

"Yeah, that's some tough shit, man," Terry lifted his cola and clinked the glass against Malcolm's. "You're a good man, you'll do the right thing. You'll figure it all out."

Malcolm took another drink, not quite realising how much of the whiskey was already gone. He savoured the burn, letting the reckless sensation wash over him. "Hah, I feel like I always want to do the right thing. But here's the thing, I didn't even tell Chloe I was coming here to drink. I just left her with the kids like an asshole. Can't even get a new job to save my life. I'm a coward."

Terry shook his head. "I don't know what to say, man," he replied. "You're not a coward. The market is rough at the moment. Not your fault, it's just the shitty hand you've been dealt."

"You don't know the half of it," Malcolm said, taking another swig. "It feels like every day will be the day things finally implode, like finding a job wasn't hard enough, like raising a family wasn't already pushing us over the edge, we're living in a constant state of perpetual fear."

"That sucks, man, I can't imagine what that's like," Terry said. "Have you thought about a job down in the mines? My brother works at the one down by Springfield. Says they're always looking for people. Hard work, long hours, long stints on site, but the pay is good. Real good."

"Shit," Malcolm said. "Sounds a lot better than anything I've been coming across lately. I'll take whatever I can get at the moment."

"I can make a call if you'd like?" Terry asked.

"That would be incredible," Malcolm said, raising his empty glass to clink Terry's. "I suppose I should call the wife back, she must be worried sick."

XXVIII

Back at home Chloe was less than impressed. She knew children put couples under a lot of new stress, but she never imagined anything like this.

She couldn't believe he would just drop off the face of the planet like that without another word. She would never put him through that worry. Her hands were shaking as she texted and called him constantly, left aggressive voicemails with the babies screaming in the background.

When he finally called her back she had no words left to say to him in the moment. She seethed in silence as he slurred his apologies, with fatigue and hunger contributing to his lack of cohesion after just one drink. Or was it a couple of drinks? He couldn't be sure how much he had or how long he had been out at Al's Toy Bar. He didn't think it had been very long at all.

After the apology he waited for her to forgive him. Silence.

He moved on to telling her about the job opportunity. He wasn't sure what she would think of the idea of him working down in the mines. The idea that he could be away from home for weeks at a time, not to mention the danger of working below ground, he wouldn't have been surprised if she shut him down.

He waited for her to do so. Or to tell him congratulations or to say "that's great news" or something. Anything.

Nothing.

He said he'd be home soon.

She hung up.

She waited.

The babies cried and all she could think of in the moment was that feeling of abandonment, of feeling hopeless and unsupported. She knew he had been through a lot, but what does it say about a person when they can't talk to those they are closest to?

She heard the car pull up and took in a deep breath. She felt like she would burst, but she couldn't tell whether it would be out of anger or relief.

"Don't you ever do that to me again," Chloe said as Malcolm walked in the door.

"I'm sorry," he said, scooping Sabrina up from the pram, knowing Chloe couldn't lash out at him with a baby in his arms.

"You'd better get that job," she said.

"So are you okay with me taking a job down in the mines?" Malcolm asked.

"No," Chloe replied. "But we don't have much of a choice, do we?"

Malcolm nodded, hoping that he wouldn't screw things up with this job.

Chloe turned around and caught a glimpse of Icarus in a moment of metamorphosis as he went from baby into a bright white bat of burning light, speeding from the lounge room to the kitchen, transitioning back with a loud bang inside the freezer, flinging the door open and sitting on the floor with a frozen steak in his mouth like nothing strange had happened at all.

Sabrina lay on a mat in the middle of the room, so far oblivious to her brother that her life continued on uninterrupted by his abnormal activity.

Chloe imagined this scene taking place at gunpoint and her child transforming into the hungry beast version of himself to decapitate those threatening his father. She felt like she wanted to get out of the house and have a drink or two herself, and she felt some of her anger towards Malcolm ebb away.

Icarus devoured the steak while his parents stood

and watched in disbelief. Chloe was stunned. Malcolm could hardly believe it himself. It didn't get easier to comprehend even after the incident with the cops.

XXIX

The next day they still hadn't had any officers knocking at their door or busting it down. Instead, they just had Icarus playfully zooming around the house while Chloe and Malcolm watched, fearful that he would break everything or hurt himself. He didn't.

As fantastic as it was to see Icarus coming into his own, transforming and flying all over the place, it quickly took its toll as his erratic movements frightened Sabrina from her sleeps, distracted her from her feeds, and every time Malcolm heard the transformative crack, he saw the headless bodies in his mind. Just standing there suspended in limbo, waiting for his memory's time to move forward and for gravity to bring one body, then the next, tumbling to the ground. But those images remained static, hanging there taunting him.

Chloe stood in the lounge room holding Sabrina, calling Malcolm's name over and over again but he was lost, stuck in that haunted dream state as one baby flew around like he was having the time of his life, and the other one screamed like crazy in her mother's arms.

He didn't know what came over him at the time or how to snap out of it, but when he finally came around Chloe's voice came in clear and sharp over the top of Sabrina's cries.

"Malcolm," she said. "Can you get the phone?"

The moment she said it he heard the ringing. Before then it was completely lost in the background noise, irrelevant.

"Hello?" he answered as Chloe took Sabrina into the bedroom and Icarus flew down the hall after them.

"Hello, is this Malcolm?" a man on the other end of the phone said.

"Yes," he replied. "Who is this?"

"The name's Rick," the man said. "I had your details passed on to me, heard you were looking for some work on the mines."

"Oh, shit, yeah. That's right. Yes," Malcolm said. "I need this. Wow. I wasn't expecting to hear from you so soon. So... What have you got?"

"Well, we've had a position open up just this week.

You'd be working every three weeks onsite, one week back home. Travel and accommodation are included."

"Okay," Malcolm said, mulling it over. He liked the sound of being out of town for three weeks right about now, keeping him occupied and giving him time to get some distance both physically and mentally from the decapitations. "What's the catch?" he asked.

He knew it would be so tough on Chloe, leaving her on her own for three weeks at a time, but it had to be done. They needed the money. He thought of how much his children would grow while he was away and he knew Sabrina would change so much, but the rate at which Icarus was changing truly amazed and scared him. Would he come back to something which resembled a two or three year old, or potentially with exponential growth, a teenager or adult?

"There's no catch, Malcolm," Rick said. "Mining is a challenging line of work. Many people give it a shot only to find out they can't handle it."

"How soon would you need me?" Malcolm asked.

"Can you start Monday?" Rick replied.

"Sure," he said. "Whatever you need."

They discussed some of the finer details of the job a while longer, assuring Malcolm that this is the necessary path to take to bring his family back to a place of stability and comfort, if such a thing was possible at all.

He clicked the phone down on the receiver and a moment later the bedroom door opened and Chloe re-emerged. He lifted Sabrina from her mother's arms and she still blubbered constantly and he kissed Sabrina on the forehead and danced around the house with her in his arms.

XXX

Neither Chloe or Malcolm had turned the tv on or checked the media for the fear of seeing the decapitated cops, how the investigation was going. The paranoia would have driven them mad when right now they just needed to hold their family together until things simmered down. If things could possibly simmer down with children like Icarus and Sabrina.

"Monday?" Chloe said. "You're leaving on Monday?" She couldn't believe he agreed to start work so soon.

"Technically I'll be leaving Sunday night," Malcolm said, "starting the job on Monday. We need this job. I know it'll be tough, but it'll make things so much better for us."

"And you'll be away for three weeks at a time?" Chloe asked.

Malcolm nodded. "The pay is good. And I'll have an entire week afterwards to spend with you."

"Great," Chloe said. She sighed. "I don't know. I understand that you need this, we need this, but... It's just all happening so quick and I don't want to be alone again and I'm tired and I'm scared and I just... I don't know if I can do it."

Malcolm pulled her into a hug. "It'll be tough," he admitted. "But you've got this. I know you've got this. It's always going to be a challenge, but we've survived this far. We will find our way."

She hugged him back. "I thought we knew what we were getting into," she said quietly. "I had no idea."

"Me too," he said with a kiss to her forehead. "Me too."

XXXI

Another day passed and still there was no report of the double police homicide, no investigators arriving at their door step. Such a crime should have been plastered all over the news, although it was possible the police were keeping it from the public because of its somewhat paranormal nature. Wild speculation with no leads, it could have been a media frenzy if there were no progress made on the investigation.

If Chloe and Malcolm weren't constantly running around the house trying to care for their babies they'd be sick with worry for the seemingly inevitable detective on the doorstep putting the evidence together to tear their family apart in the name of justice. What evidence they had was the mystery which evaded them. Malcolm was on the ground for most of the time, so he couldn't say if there were any witnesses. Certainly if there were, no one had come forward. He didn't notice anyone walking down the road nearby, no cars driving past. At least none after Icarus had fed on the two human heads, sent exploded viscera across the road. No one had stopped while Malcolm was there. He replayed all this in his head over and over and Chloe wanted to ask, wanted to know what Malcolm knew, what the chances were that someone would come forward and dob him in, or if there were evidence there that would tie him to the crime scene. She wanted to, but couldn't bring herself to squeeze that information from him. To vocalise all those details would be too much, she thought, so she let those questions stew within her.

Malcolm felt constant nausea at the thought of the cops having their lives cut drastically short. If they hadn't pulled him over. If they hadn't escalated the situation the way they did. He had no excuses for how they acted, but now they were gone. It wasn't fair how they treated him. But was it fair that they got the punishment that they did? He couldn't say. He thought of his own family and how they would carry on if he just never came home. Showed up one day dead by the side of the road.

He thought about what he would say if someone did come asking questions. What he could say. He didn't have the answers. He felt like he would probably never have the answers.

Sunday couldn't come soon enough so he could get some distance from this place.

XXXII

Darkness was no stranger to Malcolm, but now, as he stared down the tunnel of the mine it took on a very real and tangible shape. It was a place both monstrous and intense, where you brought your own light because there was no sunlight down here.

At the start of this job, as with the start of any, there was a certain calm and patience in its instruction and execution.

Do this. Don't do that. Drill here. Destroy and collect and communicate and come back. Go further. Go deeper into the void. Don't lose the light.

There was a vast network of miners like worker ants burrowing their way into the earth. For the most part they worked as a collective whole, but in the dark it was remarkably isolating, and it didn't take long before Malcolm fell in line, following the light of the worker ahead of him, the anonymous silhouette, no name or face to identify. No voice other than to communicate what was necessary. No need to clog up the tunnels with echoes.

The worker ahead of him disappeared as he rounded a corner. As Malcolm followed he was met by a pure darkness swallowing his light. The sound of Icarus screeching from the bathroom rattled through his brain, that madness which possessed him in the darkness.

As his eyes adjusted to the darkness two figures came towards him, feet crunching on the debris which formed a loose layer of crumble on the tunnel floor.

His light shone towards their heads, or where their heads would be, and he screamed a piercing and terrifying scream as the light revealed the torn and bloody stumps of two headless men in police officer uniforms.

As they came closer he knew his mind was playing these tortuous tricks on him and he reached out to touch the bodies and they fell right through him like a ghost, dissipating into thin air in the process.

He felt the sweat trickling down his neck followed by a sudden awareness that his scream still echoed through the cave like a banshee.

He reached the spot where a line of workers were

chipping away at the rock. No one seemed to notice his scream or no one seemed to care. He joined in on chipping away at the wall, adding to the chaotic percussive rhythm of the hammers eating away at the wall.

XXXIII

Chloe collapsed on the couch on the Sunday night she was left alone with the babies. She stared at them and felt the cold walls of the hospital's maternity ward creep into her mind, the sheer helplessness and overwhelming nature of that place consuming her thoughts. And everything had been a chaotic spiral since then. She couldn't tell if they were better or worse, just more chaotic, irreplaceably different. The isolation was the same, only now she had two babies to care for and and an infinitely long three week stretch of time ahead of her.

She changed Sabrina's nappy and Icarus flew around the room. She fed Sabrina by the bottle and threw chunks of meat to Icarus on the floor. When one screamed the other copied. When one fell asleep she wished the other would keep the peace going for long enough for them all to get a little rest. It never lasted long enough. The fatigue sent her slowly slipping away from sanity.

The power bill came in and Chloe felt her heart skip a beat. She would have to call the power company and request an extension until Malcolm's first paycheck came in at the end of the month. She hoped this job would be as good as Malcolm made it out to be.

Chloe could see the next three weeks unfolding ahead of her. She would be cooped up in her home the entire time, calling upon Janet to help with groceries, but mostly her time would be spent keeping Icarus in isolation from the wider world.

As each day passed she felt guilt gnawing away at her that she was stripping this poor child of a healthy social life, yet she justified it with the reasoning that society held no space for a creature like him. He was so far abnormal, a freak, destined to be outcast, the best Chloe could offer was to isolate herself and the rest of her family with him and try to build the best life she could out of it.

As much as she wanted these three weeks to come and go so quick, she knew that if Malcolm's job proved to be successful, there would be another block of three weeks after it, and on and on and this family life, these responsibilities fell on Chloe, and she saw the weight of them holding her down as she imagined an alternate universe where Malcolm never lost his job at Mickey's. While the babies screamed, while they fed, while they slept, while Sabrina started figuring out how to roll, while Icarus flew right up to Chloe and started sounding out his first words, all Chloe could think about were all the things which could have been.

If Malcolm never lost his job.

If Icarus never bit the heads off those cops.

If that projectile never landed in their back yard.

If they decided not to keep it.

If Chloe never fell pregnant in the first place.

All these mountains of scenarios forming other worlds in her head that she played out as she mothered alone and pushed through her doubts.

It was the Monday night when the phone rang and Chloe jumped.

XXXIV

Chloe thought this was the call. The police connecting the dots and finally tearing her family apart. What would she say? What would she do? The ringing echoed in her head but she was too numb to answer the call straight away. Would she let them take her vampire child away in the hopes that she and Malcolm might be able to provide a somewhat more normal life for Sabrina? She couldn't. The thought was too much. She loved Icarus as her own the moment she held him in her arms. He could eat half her face off. Hell, he could devour the whole neighbourhood and she would still love him with all her heart.

She picked up the phone but her mouth was so dry she couldn't push out a hello.

"Chloe?" the voice said from the other end.

Tears welled in her eyes as her thoughts of terror melted in the presence of a familiar voice. "Oh, Malcolm, my love, it's so good to hear from you."

"I've missed you too, my love," he replied. "I miss our babies so much. I don't know how I'm going to cope with three weeks of this. It's all I think about when I'm down in the mines."

"It's been so tough without you," Chloe said. "I feel so trapped. I feel so alone. I just want more than anything for Icarus to be a normal child. I want to be able to take him out of the house. For our children to get out and make friends."

"I know," Malcolm said. "But he's special. They both are, but Icarus is... Something else. He saved my life."

"But we repay him by keeping him locked up in the house," Chloe said. "I hate it. It just doesn't feel right."

"It will take time, but we'll figure it all out. I believe we can do that much for him," Malcolm said. "We just need to learn who we can trust and who we can't. Right now it's normal that we'd feel so alone in raising our kids. You're doing fine. We're doing fine. I love you."

"I love you too," Chloe said.

She could have stayed on the phone with Malcolm all night, but she was tired and the babies were tired too and Sabrina was hungry again and Malcolm was tired from his long and exhausting day of work. They both knew they needed the sleep but they knew too that it wouldn't come easy.

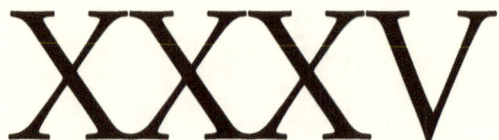

XXXV

It was the longest three weeks of her life.

Just as those first few days in the hospital seemed to stretch out forever, these weeks felt like a neverending scream.

Malcolm called every night and they talked for as long as they could, but his voice and his physical presence were two separate things.

Chloe felt like the end of the three week work cycle should have been a moment of building anticipation and excitement, but it was more of a situation where she would finally be able to get some form of relief from the exhaustion of parenthood.

A taxi pulled up into the driveway and Malcolm

climbed out. Chloe had been waiting for this moment since he had left. She opened the front door, Sabrina in her arms, and she was already struggling to hold back her tears, but the sight of her husband coming back from the mines was something else entirely. His face had sprouted a thick beard while his bald head was now covered with a thin fuzz. The bags under his eyes were sunk far deeper than she had seen before, like they too had formed the beginnings of caves.

He shouldered his bag full of dirty clothes and the taxi backed out of the driveway. Before he knew what was happening there was a loud crack and Icarus flew through the front door and landed in Malcolm's arms.

Malcolm stared at his child in bright white bat form, easily recognising those golden eyes gazing up at him.

"Holy shit," Malcolm said. "He's grown so much." He carried Icarus over to Chloe and gave her a tight hug and a kiss on the forehead. He leaned down and kissed Sabrina on the forehead too. "Sabrina has grown so much too."

They went inside and Malcolm dropped his bag in the hall.

He was so tired. She was so tired. Their duties as parents continued regardless.

Icarus squirmed out of his father's arms and transformed back into his vampire self. He crawled from the hall to the kitchen and attempted to get into the freezer.

"He's so clever," Malcolm observed.

"It makes you wonder," Chloe replied. "Where did he come from? What else is he capable of?"

Malcolm thought about it. He sure as hell couldn't come up with an answer, but he even struggled to conceive of a hypothesis, or even a wild guess as to this strange creature's origins. The thought that the sun was a dragon who spat out this infant never crossed his mind. As for what he was capable of, it seemed that question was just a more unpredictable extension of the question that gets piled on all children.

What potential.

What future lies ahead.

At what capacity do they have to exist.

What mattered right now was that this family was together. As odd as they were, as tired and frustrated and hopelessly lost as they were, this moment was their everything.

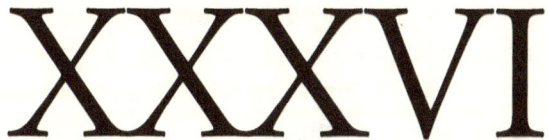

XXXVI

Before Malcolm knew what had happened, the week had passed and he was back in the mines, staring down the long, dark tunnels where every shadow looked like a haunted thing pulled from his deepest fears.

He felt like he had missed out on so much the last time he was here, it hurt so much more the second time around. He could imagine Icarus learning to talk, Sabrina learning to crawl, then to walk. He could hardly believe one of his children could fly, and that was only because he saw it with his own eyes. He could imagine his children growing and developing in leaps and bounds without him, their attachment to Chloe becoming far stronger than their bonds with him.

S. T. CARTLEDGE

He kept telling himself that this job was only temporary. It became a mantra which grew from the dark. It paid the bills. It kept the light on. It kept his family for the most part happy and healthy. But part of him felt like nothing better would come along. That he was destined to slave away in the mines while his family grew for the most part without him. He didn't know what to think or how to feel but in the distance of the tunnel there was a light which reminded him of Icarus, so he decided to focus on that.

It wasn't any easier for Chloe either, as she spent all day and all night with her children, wishing their father were home with them, knowing a large part of their family was missing. She hoped Malcolm would be able to find less demanding work by the time the children were old enough to notice he was missing and start asking why.

In Malcolm's absence she had started taking advantage of the nice weather, sitting out in the back yard, she would point to the crater in the ground which was somewhat less scorched than it was the night Icarus landed, and she would tell her children of that night, where she felt so run down, so defeated, and in that moment of difficulty and darkness, Malcolm pulled that small child from the ground. From that little ball of light Chloe told her children how she felt so much warmth and so much love, how she would never forget that moment with Malcolm standing there with Icarus crying in his arms.

S.T. Cartledge is a bizarro author and poet based in Perth, Western Australia who writes surreal dreamscapes which blur genres and stretch the imagination.